THIS BOOK BELONGS TO ZOE

The Snow Queen

Dorling DK Kindersley

LONDON, NEW YORK, SYDNEY, DELHI, PARIS MUNICH, and JOHANNESBURG

Project Editor Naia Bray Moffatt
Art Editor Catherine Goldsmith
Picture Research Liz Moore
Managing Art Editor Jacquie Guilliver
Senior Editor Marie Greenwood
DTP Designer Jill Bunyan
Production Nicola Torode

First American Edition, 2000
00 01 02 03 04 05 10 9 8 7 6 5 4 3 2 1

Published in the United States by
Dorling Kindersley Publishing, Inc.
95 Madison Avenue, New York, New York 10016

DK Publishing offers special discounts for bulk purchases for sales promotions or premiums.
Specific, large-quantity needs can be met with special editions, including personalized covers, excerpts of
existing guides, and corporate imprints. For more information, contact Special Markets Department, DK
Publishing, Inc., 95 Madison Avenue, New York, NY 10016 Fax: 800-600-9098.

Library of Congress Cataloging-in-Publication Data
Mitchell, Adrian, 1932-
    The snow queen / by Hans Andersen ; retold by Adrian Mitchell ; illustrated by
Nilesh Mistry -- 1st American ed.
        p.cm. -- (Dorling Kindersley young classics)
    Summary: When the Snow Queen abducts her friend Kai, Gerda sets out on a
perilous and magical journey to find him.
    ISBN 0-7894-6680-5
    [1. Fairy tales.] I. Andersen, H.C. (Hans Christian), 1805-1875. Snedronningen. English. II. Mistry,
Nilesh, ill. III Title. IV. Series
    PZ8.M67 Sn 2000
    839.8'l36--dc21
    [[Fic]]   00-027947

Printed in Italy by L.E.G.O.

Acknowledgements
The publisher would like to thank the following for their kind permission to
reproduce their photographs:
a=above, c-center, b=bottom, l=left, r=right, t=top
Bridgeman Art Library: 7tr, 12tl, 48tl, cl; **Bruce Coleman Collection:** 19br;
ET Archive: 47cr, 48clb; **Mary Evans Picture Library:** 38tl, 46bla, bc, 47tl, tr, 48tr;
Robert Harding Picture Library: 47br; **Kobal Collection:** 48br;
Getty Stone: 11tr, 15bl, 22br, 28bl, 30bl, 35tr.

The publisher would particularly like to thank the following people:
Adrienne Hutchinson (designer); Chris Molan (additional illustration)

See our complete catalog at
www.dk.com

YOUNG CLASSICS

The Snow Queen

By Hans Christian Andersen

Retold by Adrian Mitchell
Illustrated by Nilesh Mistry

A Dorling Kindersley Book

Contents

*

*

✳

✳

The Broken Mirror

HOLD ON TIGHT. Here we go! When we reach the end of the story, we'll all know a bit more than we know now. Once upon a time there was a demon, the worst demon in the world. Some called him Old Nick or Old Scratch, but everybody knew he was the Devil himself. One day he was really happy – he'd invented a powerful magic mirror. Anything good or beautiful reflected in this looking-glass shriveled away to nearly nothing. But everything useless or ugly looked handsome and important.

The prettiest countryside looked like boiled spinach, and the kindest people looked horrible – with upside-down heads, or with holes where their stomachs should be.

It's a really funny mirror, thought the Devil. If anybody had a kind thought, this horrible leer would appear on their reflected face, twisting it so that you couldn't recognize it.

The Devil laughed at his own cleverness. All the little imps who attended The School of Demons where the Devil was headmaster cheered their teacher. For the first time they could see what people and places really looked like. They ran all over the world with the mirror, cackling away. Finally every person in the world had been reflected in the glass and distorted by it.

One day the imps decided to fly up to heaven with the mirror to make fun of the angels. But as they carried it up through the clouds the mirror began to shake with laughter.

Up and up they flew toward the heavenly gates. But by now the mirror was shaking so hard that they lost their grip and dropped it.

The Devil's mirror hurtled down to earth and burst into a hundred million pieces.

That's when the real trouble started.

The name "devil" comes from a Greek word meaning to set one against another. The Devil's mirror in this story sets people against each other by making people see the ugly side of things.

Some pieces were no bigger than grains of sand, and the wind blew these all over the planet.

If a grain of that mirror-glass lodged in somebody's eye, it stayed there. Then that person saw everything falsely and could only see the ugly side of things and people.

The most terrible thing of all was when a splinter of the glass entered somebody's heart. That heart became just like a lump of solid ice.

Some pieces of mirror were so large that they were made into windowpanes. But it was best not to look at your friends through windows like that.

Some medium-size pieces were fitted into eyeglasses—you can imagine what happened if you wanted a fair trial and the judge put on glasses like that.

All this made the Devil laugh so much that his stomach split. He was, as they say, tickled to death.

But some pieces of devil-glass were still floating and spinning through the air. Listen to what happened next.

The mirror hurtled down to earth and burst into a hundred million pieces.

Best Friends

THE BIG TOWN is so crowded that many families can't have a garden. They make do with a few flowerpots. But there was once a poor girl and poor boy who shared a rooftop garden of their own. They weren't brother and sister, but best friends. Their families lived in the attics of two tall houses, and their windows faced each other.

You could step out of one window, hop over the gutter, cross a small flat roof, and in through your best friend's window. On that roof were wooden boxes full of earth for growing herbs for cooking with and rose-trees for looking at.

So that was the garden where the children played. Sweet peas dangled over the side of the boxes and two rose-trees twined round the windows and formed a little green arch. There the two friends sat together, on little stools underneath the roses, telling each other stories and inventing wonderful games.

When winter came, the rooftop garden was too cold for playing. The windows were sealed tight and often frosted over. Then the children heated copper coins on stoves and pressed them against the ice windowpanes to make two round peepholes.

One friendly eye looked out from each peephole. One was the little boy's, one was the little girl's. His name was Kai, which rhymes with sky, and hers was Gerda. In summertime they could reach each other with one jump onto the rooftop. But in winter they had to run down seven flights of stairs, across a snowy courtyard, and up another seven flights of stairs to meet each other.

"The white bees are swarming again," said the old Grandmother.

"Do they have a queen?" asked Kai, for he knew that every beehive has its queen.

"Yes, the snow-bees have a queen," said Grandmother. "The Snow Queen. On winter nights she often glides through the streets of the town. She stares in at every window and leaves icy flower patterns on the windowpanes."

"Could the Snow Queen come in here?" asked Gerda.

"Just let her try," said Kai. "I'll stick her on a red-hot stove and she'll melt away to a puddle."

Grandmother patted his head and changed the subject by telling another story.

That evening, when Kai was home and ready for bed, he stood on a chair and gazed out through the round peephole in his window. He saw one snowflake the size of a cup falling onto the roof. As he watched, the snowflake grew and grew until it became a tall woman.

She wore a white gown, woven from millions of tiny snowflakes. She was very beautiful, she was all glittering, blinding ice.

But she was alive. Her eyes looked at Kai like two bright stars – but there was no peace or kindness in them. She nodded to the window and beckoned to him.

Kai was so scared that he jumped off his chair. And it seemed to him that a great bird flew past the window.

When winter came, the rooftop garden was too cold for playing.

Next day was frosty and clear. The sun woke up and stretched his rays – and the thaw began. Soon it was green springtime. Gerda and Kai sat in their garden again, high above the town.

Summertime came and the roses were glowing. Kai and Gerda sat looking at an animal picture book. Suddenly, just as the churchtower struck five o'clock, Kai shouted: "Oh! There's a pain in my heart. Ow! There's something in my eye!"

"Let me look," said Gerda. "Blink your eyelids up and down. It'll make them water and wash out whatever it is. Let me see, Kai." She held up his eyelid and gazed. "I can't see anything at all."

"It must have gone or melted away," said Kai. "It was like a grain of glass in my eye and a splinter of glass in my heart."

But those two flying pieces of the Devil's mirror hadn't gone or melted away. One was changing Kai's eyesight, so that everything good looked ugly. The other was turning Kai's heart into a lump of solid ice. One second later he was changed utterly.

Kai picked up a stick and slashed the head off the rose.

"Keep away from me!" he screeched at Gerda.

Gerda jumped back as if she'd been stung by a wasp. "Kai! Did I hurt you?"

Kai mimicked her voice cruelly: "'Kai! Did I hurt you?' Keep your clammy hands away from me.

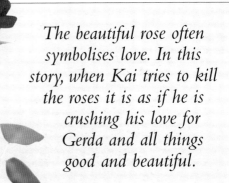

The beautiful rose often symbolises love. In this story, when Kai tries to kill the roses it is as if he is crushing his love for Gerda and all things good and beautiful.

They're all pink and sweaty. Your fingers look like moldy sausages."

"Why are you talking like that? Did something hurt you?" asked Gerda.

"Course not, you stupid little girl. But it hurts me to look at you. You're ugly as a bullfrog. Aren't you going to cry? Why don't you cry? Then you'll look twice as ugly."

"We never cry," said Gerda, gulping. "I never cry."

"We'll see about that," said Kai, grinning nastily.

"You're not Kai," said Gerda. "I'm asleep in my bed. You're a nightmare boy who looks like Kai. I want to wake up."

Kai laughed: "I'll wake you up, don't you worry. Look at this rose. Disgusting. It's crawling with scaly worms."

Kai picked up a stick and slashed the head off the rose.

"They're horrible roses," he said, "I'll kill them all."

He raised his stick again, but Gerda grabbed it and broke it in two. "Sit down, Kai," she said. "Sit down and think. You're ill. Think about what you're doing."

"All I can think about is what a squeaky, scratchy voice you've got. Sounds like a cat being boiled alive. I don't want to be here on this stupid rooftop." He broke off another rose, crushed it with his foot, turned his back on Gerda, and climbed back into his attic.

Gerda covered her face in her hands. "We're best friends," she kept telling herself. "I'm sure he'll get better. Whatever happens, we're best friends."

But Kai didn't get better. Kind Kai had changed into cruel Kai. If Gerda came to him with a picture book, he told her picture books were for babies and tore its pages. If Grandmother tried to tell one of her marvelous stories he would laugh at the sad parts and make faces behind her back.

When Hans Andersen was a child in Denmark, sleds were the main form of transport during the long winters. But then, as now, children preferred toboggans!

One winter day, as snow was falling, Kai produced a magnifying glass to inspect the snowflakes settling on his blue coat.

"Look through this glass, Gerda," he said. "See how cunning these snowflakes are. One like a splendid orchid. One like a ten-pointed star. Much more interesting than flowers. If they didn't have to melt, they'd be perfect in every way."

Gerda liked flowers better, but she was too scared of Kai's sharp tongue to say so. So she just smiled.

"What's that stupid smile for?" said Kai. "I'm going tobogganing down in the Square – and you can't come with me."

Down at the Square the bravest boys often tied their toboggans behind the farmers' carts and zipped along behind them over the snow.

Suddenly the white sled stopped.

In the middle of all the fun, a great white sled, drawn by a black horse and a white horse, drove up. In the sled sat a tall figure, all wrapped up in a white fur coat and wearing a white fur hat.

The sled circled the Square twice. Kai managed to fasten his toboggan to it, so that he was pulled along behind.

Faster and faster they went, down the darkening streets of the town. The driver of the sled gave Kai a nod as if they knew each other. Each time Kai thought of unhooking his toboggan, the driver gave another nod, so he stayed where he was.

Out of the town they drove and the snow fell thick and fast.

"Stop! I want to go home!" he yelled, but nobody heard him. The snow swirled down and the sled flew onward.

Now and then it gave a jump, as if they were crossing hedges and ditches. Kai was terrified – he tried to pray, but all he could remember was his multiplication tables.

"Five fives are twenty-five, five sixes are thirty, five sevens are thirty-five, five eights are eighty – no, that's not right. Oh!..." Suddenly the white sled stopped. The driver stood up, in a coat and hat of purest snow. She was a woman, tall and glittering. She was the Snow Queen.

"We've come a long way," said the Snow Queen to the shivering Kai. "But you look so cold. Cuddle down into my polar bearskin coat." She put her furs around him. It was like sinking down into a snowdrift.

"Are you still cold?" she asked, and kissed him on the forehead.

Her kiss was colder than any ice. It went straight to Kai's icy heart. For a moment he felt – I'm dying! But soon he found that he didn't feel the cold any more.

"My toboggan! Don't forget my toboggan!" he said. The Snow Queen gave Kai another kiss. He felt as if he were drowning in a sea of diamonds. Memories of his toboggan, his parents, Grandmother, and Gerda became lost in that diamond mist. Another moment and he couldn't remember anything about them.

"Do I get a third kiss?" asked Kai.

"You mustn't have any more kisses," said the Snow Queen, "or I shall kiss you to death."

Kai's journey with the Snow Queen through angry blizzards reflects the coldness in the Snow Queen's heart. Kai, too, has lost his warm heart and can only remember "cold" facts.

Kai looked up at her. She was very beautiful. He said: "I think you are perfect. I'm not afraid of you now. I hope you like me. People think I'm bright. I can do addition in my head, multiplication and division. I can even do fractions. I can tell you how many square miles there are in Spain or Denmark or the USA. I know the population of Timbuktu and Omsk and Tomsk. I know how long the Amazon is and the Mississippi and the exact height of every famous mountain and volcano."

"That's good," said the Snow Queen.

She put her furs around him.

"But perhaps that's not really enough?"
he asked doubtfully.

"Perhaps," she said. "We shall see. But now
we must be on our way." She cracked a whip and called
to her two horses. "Giddyup, Moonlight! Giddyup, Midnight!"

The Snow Queen smiled at Kai and he looked up into the
great darknesses of the sky as they swept along on the crest
of a black cloud.

They flew over woods and lakes, over land and sea. Below them
angry blizzards raged and lean wolves howled. But high above
everything else there shone the perfect silver moon.

Kai gazed up at that moon all through the long winter night.
But all the next day he slept at the feet of the Snow Queen.

Gerda's Quest

HOURS PASSED, days passed, weeks passed and still Kai hadn't come home. Nobody knew where he'd gone. The boys in the Square could only say they'd seen Kai's toboggan speeding out of the town behind a fine white sled.

Everybody was sorry and many were sad, but Gerda cried her heart out. People began to say Kai must be dead, probably drowned in the winding river. It was a long and miserable winter.

Then spring swung around again, and the sun shone down.

"Kai's dead and gone," said Gerda.

"I don't believe it," said the sunshine.

"He is dead and gone, isn't he?" she asked the swallows.

"We don't believe it either," said the swallows and in the end Gerda began to think that Kai was still alive.

"I'm going to find Kai, wherever he is," said Gerda to the sunshine and the swallows. "I'll put on my new red shoes, the shoes that Kai has never seen. And then I'll go down to that old winding river and ask her a few questions."

Early next morning she kissed her Grandmother, who was still asleep, put on her red shoes, and walked out of the town down to the riverside. She sang to the river:

Winding river, many people say
You have taken my friend away.
Winding river, give me back my friend
And if you'll bring him back again –
You shall have my red shoes, you shall have
my pretty shoes,
You shall have my pretty red shoes.

The small waves on the river seemed to nod to her, so Gerda took off her red shoes and threw them into the water. They splashed in not far from the bank. The little waves brought them straight back to her.

Perhaps I didn't throw my shoes far enough, thought Gerda. So she climbed into a little boat lying among the rushes, clambered along to the far end of it, then stood up and threw the shoes as far as she possibly could.

But the boat wasn't tied up. Gerda's throw set it drifting away from the bank and downstream. She didn't notice she was afloat until it was too late to jump ashore. Gerda was frightened. The sparrows tried to comfort her by chirping, "Here we are! Here we are!" and flying alongside her. The boat drifted onward with the red shoes floating behind it.

The river's banks were pretty with weeping willows leaning over the water gazing at their own reflections, thousands of bright wildflowers in all colors and friendly-looking sheep and cows grazing on grassy slopes. But there weren't any people in sight.

"Maybe the river will carry me to Kai," thought Gerda, and that cheered her up. She stood up and gazed around her at the green river valley and the blue and white sky.

The boat drifted onward.

The old woman hauled Gerda to safety.

Gerda's boat floated slowly by a cherry orchard. In the middle of it stood a cottage with odd red, blue, and yellow windows, a thatched roof, and two tall soldiers outside.

Gerda called out to them, but they said nothing because they were made of wood. She shouted louder and out of the cottage came an old woman, leaning on a crooked stick. She wore a sun-hat big as a cartwheel, painted with beautiful flowers.

"Old lady!" cried Gerda. "Please help me, I'm lost!"

The old woman reached out with her crooked stick, hooked its handle over the prow of the boat, and hauled Gerda to safety.

"Poor child!" she said. "How do you come to be riding on this great winding river, far from home in the wide, wide world?"

Gerda had planned an answer to this question: "My name is Gerda. I had a best friend named Kai. But he disappeared last winter.

My friend is very sick so I must find him and make him better." She added, "I thought the river might have carried him away, so I was following the river."

"He hasn't come past here, not yet," said the old woman. "But everybody travels down this river, sooner or later. Gerda, don't look so sad. Come into my cottage and eat some of my crimson cherries."

She led Gerda into the cottage. The sunlight shone in strangely through the red and blue and yellow windows. But on the table was a bowl of glowing cherries.

"Eat as many as you like. I've always longed for a nice little girl like you," said the old woman.

"I must be on my way soon," said Gerda, "I must find Kai."

"Of course," said the old woman. "But while you're eating your cherries I'll comb your hair with my special golden comb."

But the comb was a magic comb and as her hair was being combed Gerda gradually forgot all about Kai. The old woman wasn't wicked, but she thought that Gerda might stay and keep her company if she forgot Kai.

The old woman slipped out into the garden. She pointed her crooked stick at each of her rose-trees. They all sank down into the dark earth, out of sight. If Gerda saw the roses, she might think of the roses in her rooftop garden at home – and then she would remember Kai and run away.

The old woman bustled into the cottage and showed Gerda where to sleep – in a swansdown bed with red silk pillows filled with blue violets. There she slept sweetly and dreamed happily for the first time since Kai vanished.

Blue violets represent faithfulness. The old woman has put these flowers in Gerda's pillow, so that she will forget about finding Kai and be faithful to her.

Next morning Gerda explored the garden, which seemed to have every kind of flower. She played in the garden every day of a summer which seemed to go on forever. The flowers were talkative and friendly, but Gerda sometimes had a strange feeling that there was a flower missing.

One day she was looking at the old woman's sun-hat with the painted flowers, and the prettiest of all was – a rose. Roses!

"What?" said Gerda. "No roses?" She inspected every flowerbed, but there wasn't a single rose. She sat down and cried just one tear, but that tear fell where a rose-tree had sunk, and its warmth brought the tree sprouting up and blooming. Gerda hugged the tree and kissed its roses as she remembered the roses on her rooftop, as she remembered her best friend – Kai!

"I've been wasting time," she said. "I'm supposed to be searching for Kai! Do you know where Kai is?" she asked the roses. "Do you think he's dead and gone?"

The rosebush sang to her, in a rosy voice as soft as petals:

"I have been deep down under the ground.
Where the bony dead are found.
Kai was not with them, Kai was not there.
Kai is still alive in the open, open air.
Kai is still alive – somewhere!"

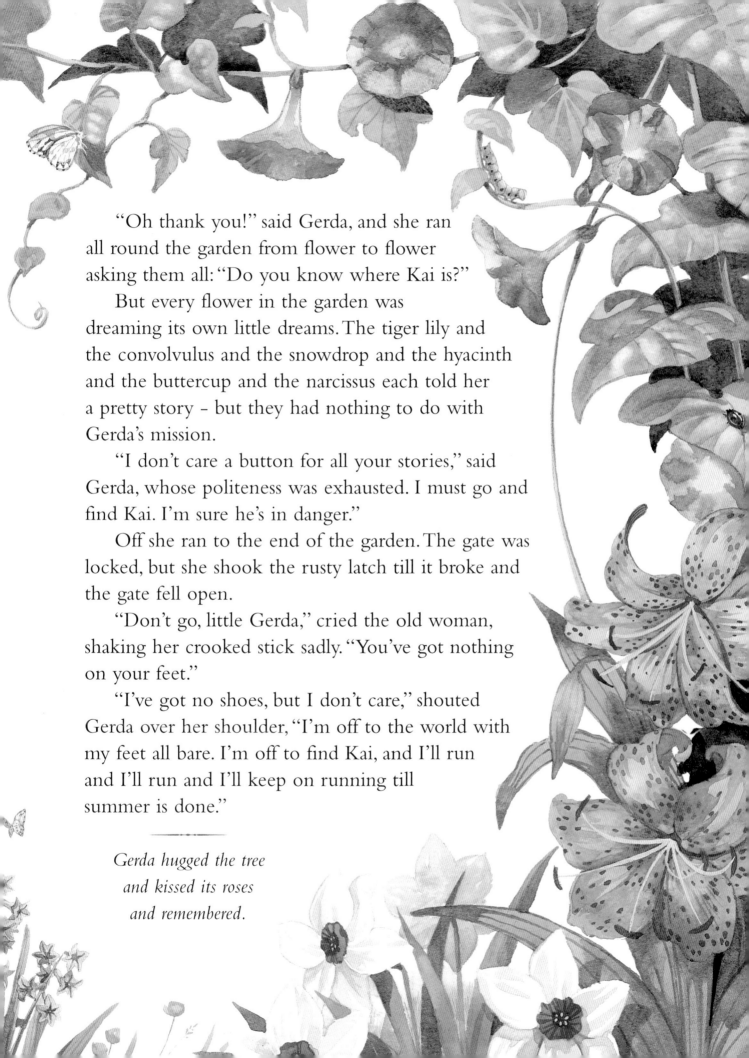

"Oh thank you!" said Gerda, and she ran all round the garden from flower to flower asking them all: "Do you know where Kai is?"

But every flower in the garden was dreaming its own little dreams. The tiger lily and the convolvulus and the snowdrop and the hyacinth and the buttercup and the narcissus each told her a pretty story – but they had nothing to do with Gerda's mission.

"I don't care a button for all your stories," said Gerda, whose politeness was exhausted. I must go and find Kai. I'm sure he's in danger."

Off she ran to the end of the garden. The gate was locked, but she shook the rusty latch till it broke and the gate fell open.

"Don't go, little Gerda," cried the old woman, shaking her crooked stick sadly. "You've got nothing on your feet."

"I've got no shoes, but I don't care," shouted Gerda over her shoulder, "I'm off to the world with my feet all bare. I'm off to find Kai, and I'll run and I'll run and I'll keep on running till summer is done."

Gerda hugged the tree and kissed its roses and remembered.

Meet the Crow

GERDA RAN and ran and ran. At last she couldn't run any more, so she sat down on a rock. She looked around and realized summer was over.

"I have to move on," said Gerda. "The air's getting colder, and here comes the snow –"

"And here comes the Crow!" Hopping up to her, a large crow, who had been watching Gerda for some time, greeted her.

"Caw-de-caw! Caw-de-caloo! Caw-de-caw – and how d'you do?"

"I'm not doing very well, thank you," said Gerda.

The Crow clacked his beak. "I can see that, Caw-de-caw! A small girl out in the wide world, feet all bare and all alone."

"All alone except for you, kind Crow."

"Caw-de-caloo, so who are you?"

Gerda recited the reasons for her quest: "My name is Gerda. I had a best friend named Kai, but he disappeared last winter. My friend is very sick, so I must find him and make him better. Have you seen him?"

The Crow nodded wisely. "Maybe I have! Maybe!"

"He's alive! Kai's alive!" cried Gerda, giving the Crow a bear-hug and kissing his feathers.

"Now hold your hummingbirds!" said the Crow. "You're just about to squooze me to death. This Kai, does he have the gleam of a mountain eagle in his eye?"

"Oh, yes," cried Gerda.

The Danish word for crow is "kragemaal" which means "gibberish". The crow in this story talks gibberish or "Double Dutch".

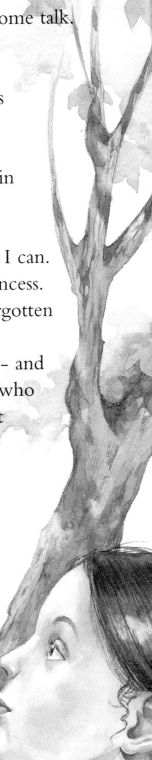

"That's Kai. Did you hear him talk? Did he sound clever?"

The Crow considered this. "I heard him talk some talk. He was as clever as clockwork."

"Kai!" said Gerda.

"Well, he'll have forgotten about you now he's found his princess," said the Crow flatly.

"Does he live with a princess?" asked Gerda.

"Listen," said the Crow. "But it's hard to explain in people language. Can you speak Crow?"

"I'm sorry, I never learned how," said Gerda.

"Never mind," said the Crow, "I'll do the best I can. Er hem. This country has an amazingly clever Princess. She's read all the newspapers in the world and forgotten them all. That's how flapping clever she is.

"The other day she was sitting on her throne – and she thought to herself: I want to be married, but who to? I want a husband with a mind of his own, not some handsome waxwork. It's all true," said the Crow. "My sweetheart's a Tame Crow who lives in the palace."

"Yes, I believe you," said Gerda impatiently.

"Good," said the Crow. "Well, the newspapers printed the Princess's picture on their front pages with a frame of little hearts and announced: any good-looking young man can come to the palace and talk with the Princess. And she'll decide who is the best talker – and marry him right away."

Gerda recited the reasons
for her quest.

"The Princess would marry the best talker?" asked Gerda.

"Caw-rect," said the Crow. "Anyway – crowds of young men appeared. They could talk well enough out in the street, but in the palace – with its guards in silver armor at the door and flunkies in gold braid on the marble stairs and diamond chandeliers glittering in the great ballroom – well, they got flustered, flummoxed, and speechless. They all failed on the first two days.

"Of course, when they were out in the street again they gabbled so fast that you couldn't hear yourself croak."

"But Kai, little Kai!" said Gerda. "When did he arrive?"

"Give me time!" said the Crow. "I'm just coming to him. On the third day a little fellow strode right up to the palace, bold as a buzzard. His eyes were bright like yours and he had fine, long hair, but his clothes were raggedy."

"That was Kai! I've found him at last!"

She was sitting on a pearl the size of a spinning wheel.

"There was a knapsack on his back," said the Crow.

"No, that must have been his toboggan," said Gerda.

"Maybe, maybe not," said the Crow huffily. "What's the difference? But I know from my sweetheart that when he saw the guards in silver armor at the door and the flunkies in gold braid on the marble stairs, he just gave them a friendly nod and walked on into the ballroom.

"The diamond chandeliers were all ablaze. Ministers of State and Ambassadors were walking about in their bare feet, carrying golden dishes to and fro. The boy's boots squeaked dreadfully, but that didn't seem to bother him."

"It must be Kai," said Gerda. "He did have new boots – I remember them squeaking."

"Well, they squeaked like a pocketful of mice!" said the Crow. "But he marched up to the Princess. She was sitting on a pearl the size of a spinning wheel."

"Did Kai win the Princess?" asked Gerda.

"Look, if I hadn't been a crow, I'd have won her myself, even though I am engaged. He was handsome, like me, and clever as a clarinet. He hadn't come to woo the Princess, but just to listen to her wise talking. And he liked her, and she liked him."

"Of course it was Kai," said Gerda. "He always was clever. He could do addition in his head and even fractions. Oh, please take me to that palace."

"Easier said than done," said the Crow. "I'll talk to my fiancée about it. She'll know best. They won't let a little girl like you just walk into the palace."

"As soon as Kai hears I'm outside, he'll run out and fetch me," said Gerda.

"Wait for me on this rock," said the Crow. He waggled his head and flew away.

It was late evening before the Crow returned. "Caw-de-caw!" he croaked. "My fiancée says she'll get you into the palace. She knows a little backstair leading to the Royal Bedroom."

So the Crow led Gerda through the palace gardens, along a mile-long avenue lined with giant trees, and round the splendid palace to a little open door at the back near the kitchens.

By the light of a small oil lamp at the bottom of the stairs she saw the Crow's sweetheart. "My fiancé speaks highly of you, young lady," said the Tame Crow. "Carry the illumination, please, and I will lead the way."

Gerda picked up the lamp and followed the Tame Crow through a maze of beautiful rooms. The Wild Crow shuffled along nervously behind Gerda.

Finally the three of them stood in the doorway of the Royal Bedroom.

The ceiling was like a great palm-tree with leaves of crystal. In the middle of the room was a tall gold stem and from it hung two beds, like lilies. One of the beds was white; the Princess was sleeping in that one.

The other bed was crimson, and it was there that Gerda ran to look for Kai. She turned back one of the crimson petals, and there he was!

Gerda called Kai's name aloud. She held the little oil lamp close to his head. The boy woke up, and turned his head and – it wasn't Kai!

"What's happening?" called the Princess.

Gerda gulped, then told them her whole story, and all that the crows had done for her.

"You poor girl!" said the Prince and Princess. They praised the crows and said they would be rewarded.

"Would you like to fly away and be free birds?" asked the Princess. "Or would you rather be appointed Crows to the Court and be paid with all the scraps from the kitchen?"

The two crows bowed deeply, and asked to be appointed to the Court. "Silver feathers among the black, you know," said the Wild Crow. "We're not getting any younger. Should put something by for a wormless day."

The Prince climbed out of his bed and let Gerda sleep in it. She folded her hands and thought, how kind birds and people are! Then she closed her eyes and fell asleep.

Next day Gerda was dressed by the ladies-in-waiting in silk and velvet from head to foot, with boots and a fur muff. The Prince and the Princess helped her into a carriage of pure gold and wished her farewell and good luck. There were four horses and a coachman, a footman, and outriders. The Tame Crow and the Wild Crow stood in the palace gateway, flapping goodbye as long as they could still see the coach, glittering like the sun on wheels.

The three of them stood in the doorway of the Royal Bedroom.

The Robbers' Castle

ROLLING ALONG through the heart of a dark forest, Gerda's carriage shone so brightly that the gang of Robbers lurking in ambush were dazzled.

"Gold! Gold!" they screamed, charging out of the bushes. They grabbed the horses' reins, killed the coachman, footman, and outriders, and dragged Gerda from the coach.

"She's lovely and plump, she's been fattened on nuts," said an old robber woman called Muz with a grizzly beard. "I'll eat her roasted, the little lamb." And she drew a knife like rusty lightning.

"Aoow!" she screamed. Her ear was being bitten by Buzzer, her little daughter who was riding on her back.

"She'll be my friend and play with me," yelled Buzzer. "She'll give me her beautiful princess cloak. And sleep in my bed with me. D'you agree, old Muz?" And she chewed her mother's ear again.

"Aoow!" cried Muz. "Agreed!"

Buzzer jumped down, and pulled Gerda into the coach. The robber gang drove deeper into the forest.

The robber girl put her arm around Gerda. "Don't you worry. I won't let them kill you. You're a princess, aren't you?"

"No," said Gerda, "I'm just a poor girl from the town." And she told Buzzer of her search for Kai.

The robber girl nodded and said again, "I won't let them kill you – even if you do make me angry. No, I'll do the job myself!"

The coach was driven right into the robbers' castle. Through ragged holes in the walls, ravens and bats flew in and out.

Moo is Buzzer's tame reindeer. Reindeer, now only found in the far north, are the only type of deer that can be tamed.

In the middle of the floor crackled a smoky fire.

"You sleep here with me and my pets," said Buzzer, dragging Gerda over to a heap of straw. She pointed to a wooden cage high on the wall. "Those are my wild wood pigeons. And here's my old darling, Moo."

She grabbed the antlers of an old reindeer and pulled him to his feet. "I ties him up, or he'd go sneaking off. You know, every blessed evening I tickles his neck for him with my little snickersnee."

Buzzer drew her snickersnee, a jagged little knife, from her belt and demonstrated.

"Does Moo like that?" asked Gerda doubtfully.

"Oh no, he don't like that at all," laughed Buzzer as Moo backed off as far as he could. "All right – time for bed." She pulled Gerda down on to the straw.

"Do you always take your snickersnee to bed with you?" asked Gerda.

"Oh yes," said Buzzer. "You never know what might happen to you ... Tell me about Kai again," she asked, for Buzzer loved stories.

As Gerda told her the robber girl fell asleep, clutching her knife in her hand. Gerda couldn't even close her eyes. Was she going to live or die?

"Does Moo like that?"
asked Gerda doubtfully.

Suddenly one of the wood-pigeons cooed:

"Roo-cool! Roo-cool! We have seen Kai glide

Through the icicle woods at the Snow Queen's side."

Gerda sat up. Buzzer was snoring. "Where was the Snow Queen taking him?" asked Gerda.

The wood-pigeon answered: "Roo-cool! Roo-cool! She must have been making for Lapland, for that land's all covered in snow. Ask the reindeer tied to the foot of the bed, for the reindeer's bound to know."

"Moo, do you know Lapland?" asked Gerda.

"Lapland?" whispered the reindeer. "Yes – great white skies and prairies glowing with golden moss. The Snow Queen lives there in summer, but her real palace is up near the North Pole on the island of white winds they call Spitzbergen."

"Poor Kai!" said Gerda.

"Lie still, Gerda, or you'll get my knife in your gizzard," said Buzzer, and Gerda obeyed. But next morning she told Buzzer everything the wood-pigeon had told her.

The robber girl looked serious, then she said: "Never mind, we'll manage. Moo, do you know where Lapland is?"

The reindeer's eyes sparkled. "That's where I was born."

"Listen Gerda," said Buzzer. "All the men have gone off to rob, leaving Muz on guard. But soon she'll take a drink from her big brass bottle, and have a little nap. That's when it'll happen."

Buzzer jumped out of bed, hugged her mother, tugged her moustachios and said: "Good morning my own darling nanny-goat!" Her mother replied with a loving punch on the nose.

The Northern lights are dazzling displays of color that light up the sky in the far north. Caused by explosions on the sun, they make the sky look as if it is on fire.

Away flew the reindeer, through forests and swamps.

As soon as Muz had drunk from her big brass
bottle and dozed off, Buzzer patted her reindeer and
said: "Moo, you know I'm itching to tickle your neck with my
snickersnee. But I'm going to cut your rope and set you free.
Carry Gerda through Lapland to the Snow Queen's palace and
her best friend."

The reindeer jumped for joy. Buzzer helped Gerda on to his back
and strapped her on tight. "You're all right, now," she said. "Keep
your fur boots and gloves – you'll need 'em. But I keep the cloak."

Then Buzzer opened the door and slashed the reindeer's rope
with her snickersnee. "Off you go, Moo!" she yelled. "But take real
good care of that girl."

Away flew the reindeer, through forests and swamps and over
great plains. Wolves howled and ravens raved. Red lights shivered
up above them, as though the whole sky was trying to sneeze.

"Those are the good old Northern Lights," said the happy
reindeer. "How's that for shining!"

Then he ran onward faster than ever, by day and night, till
suddenly he stopped, lifted his great head and sniffed the air
deeply. "We're here," said Moo. "Welcome to Lapland!"

The Lapp Woman and the Finnish Woman

IT WAS GERDA who spotted the hut. The roof touched the ground and the doorway was so low that you had to crawl in and out.

Nobody was home except an old Lapp woman, busily frying fish on an oil stove. Moo told her his own life story first and then a few words about Gerda's quest, which seemed less important. Gerda herself was too cold to speak.

"You poor creatures!" said the Lapp woman. "You've got hundreds of snowy miles to go to find the Palace of the Snow Queen. I'll write you a letter to my friend who lives near there, an old Finnish woman. Show it to her, she'll know what to do. I've no writing paper so I'll have to write on a nice piece of dried cod."

Gerda cheered up after something to drink and eat. The Lapp woman wrote a few thousand words on the dried cod, gave it to Gerda, tied her on the reindeer and off they went again.

Soon they were knocking on the chimney of the old Finnish woman, for she didn't even have a door.

It was hot as Africa inside. The old woman took off Gerda's gloves and boots and cooled the reindeer's forehead with ice.

The Lapp woman wrote a few thousand words.

Then she read her dried cod three times, learning it by heart, and popped the codfish into her soup-kettle – waste not, want not. "Now I know everything about you," said the Finnish woman.

"I can tell you're magic, madam," said the reindeer. "Won't you give Gerda a potion that will grant her the strength of ten men, so that she can overcome the Snow Queen?"

The Finnish woman laughed. "The strength of ten men? That wouldn't get her very far." She took down an ancient parchment from her scroll-shelf, unrolled it, and read its magical hieroglyphics till sweat poured down her forehead.

Then she drew the reindeer into the corner, and whispered: "Kai is with the Snow Queen at her Palace. He believes she's kind and beautiful; but that's because of the devil-glass in his heart and his eye. These bits must come out and come out quickly, or Kai will never be human again and the Snow Queen will keep him forever."

"Can't you give the girl a magic spell to free Kai?"

"I can't give Gerda any more power than she has already. Don't you see how strong that is? Look how people and animals all want to help her? See how far she's traveled through this harsh world on her bare feet?

"But she mustn't know where her power lies. It springs from the innocence of her heart. Gerda alone can save Kai.

"Quick! Carry her to the Snow Queen's garden ten miles from here. But you must leave her when you come to a red berry bush in the snow. Now, off you go!"

The Finnish woman
lifted Gerda onto the reindeer's back. Off
galloped Moo through the door and over the snow.
"I've forgotten my boots and gloves!" called
Gerda. But Moo didn't dare stop till he came
to the red berry bush. There he put down
Gerda, and nuzzled her on the nose.

"I'm not allowed to come any
farther," he said.

"Who makes cruel rules like that?"

"I don't know," said Moo, "but they
mustn't be broken. Never break a rule until
you know what can be done with the pieces."

Gerda stroked the reindeer's neck and
whispered a song into his left ear:

"The world's so big, and we two so small,
It often seems we don't matter at all.
But your heart is so true and your
courage so strong,
I'm sure as the sun that we'll meet before long —
This year, next year, sometime, sometime soon."

Then Moo turned and dashed away, with
reindeer tears rolling down his cheeks.

There stood Gerda, all alone, in
the middle of a terrible land of ice
and snow. She began to run forward
on her blue bare feet.

Suddenly an army of snowflakes appeared in front of her. They didn't fall from the sky – for that was cloudless – they marched along the ground. The nearer they came, the bigger they grew. Gerda remembered how huge the snowflakes had looked through Kai's magnifying glass. But these were much bigger and more frightening.

As Kai discovers, every snowflake has its own unique shape. Here the snowflakes have terrifying shapes to become an evil army.

These snowflakes were alive! They were the Snow Queen's soldiers and their shapes were monstrous. Some were like hideous giant porcupines, others like cobras knotted together, some like grizzly bears with spiky fur. They were so brightly white they made you shut your eyes.

Gerda recited a prayer her Grandmother had taught her. The air was so cold she could see the words floating out of her mouth in letters of smoke.

This smoke thickened and formed itself into a cloud of small, shining angels, all of them with helmets on their heads and spears and shields in their hands. As the cloud touched the ground, the angels grew taller, and more and more of them appeared until Gerda was surrounded by an army of angels. They flung their spears at the monster snowflakes, breaking them into a hundred thousand pieces.

The angels breathed on Gerda's feet and hands, so she hardly felt the cold any more as she walked quickly on toward the Palace of the Snow Queen.

These snowflakes were alive!

The Palace of the Snow Queen

THE SNOW QUEEN'S PALACE stood like a towering iceberg in a sea of ice. It held a maze of one hundred rooms, carved by blizzards from the drifting snow.

At its center was a great and deadly cavern. Its floor was a frozen lake of black ice. This ice was cracked into thousands of pieces. And each piece looked exactly like all the other pieces.

In the middle of the dark floor stood the throne of the Snow Queen. She called her lake The Mirror of Reason – the only truthful mirror in the world.

Little Kai was stumbling around on this ice. He felt no cold, for the Queen had kissed away all his shivering.

He was dragging flat pieces of ice around, trying to join them together to make a word. He was surrounded by a vast and probably impossible puzzle in which all the pieces were the same.

"How goes the Great Game of Reason, Kai?" asked the Snow Queen quietly from her throne.

"It's very difficult," said Kai. "It's like trying to do a jigsaw puzzle in your head."

"But it's much more important than a jigsaw puzzle, isn't it?" said the Queen.

"Oh yes," said Kai, because she had taught him well. "It's the most important thing of all. The only thing that matters is the Great Game."

"That's right. It's the only thing that matters. You must put the pieces together to form the word."

"I must put the pieces together to form a word," said Kai.

The Queen stood in her fury. "Not a word, you stupid boy! *The* word! Has your brain gone numb?"

"I must put the pieces together to form the word."

"And what is the word?" screamed the Snow Queen.

"The word I must make with the pieces is – ETERNITY."

The Queen relaxed into her tall, cold throne. "ETERNITY, yes. And what does ETERNITY mean?"

"I think it means – forever."

"Very good, Kai, very good," said the Queen. "If you can make that word – ETERNITY – you shall be free and I will give you the whole world – and a pair of skates."

"It's very difficult," said Kai.

"It's meant to be difficult," said the Queen. "Now I must fly away to whiten the peaks of my volcanoes. Work hard at the Great Game, Kai. I'll be back in a heartbeat."

Kai was left staring at the thousands of pieces of ice, and thinking, thinking, thinking until he had thought himself dizzy. He sat there on the black ice, not moving a muscle. You might have thought he had been frozen to death.

"And what is the word?" screamed the Snow Queen.

Ice skating, performed mostly on frozen rivers or lakes, was very popular. A new pair of skates would have been a great treat.

Gerda walked into the Palace through the great gate of piercing winds. She walked on and on through the maze of one hundred snow-drifting rooms until at last she stepped onto the throneroom's lake of ice.

There was Kai!

She knew him. She ran to him across the miles of black ice and threw her arms around him and hugged him tight and held him and cried out: "Kai! Kai! I've found you at last!"

But Kai just knelt there on the floor, cold and still as a statue of dark blue ice, silent as a stone.

"Kai!" whispered Gerda in his ear. "It's Gerda, don't you remember me? I'm not going to cry," said Gerda. "We never cry, do we?" Kai's blue lips said nothing. Then Gerda did cry. She cried only one tear, but it fell on Kai's chest.

Immediately Kai threw back his head and clutched his chest. "My heart!" he cried. "Something's happening in my heart!" And that splinter of devil-glass melted away and that lump of solid ice in his chest turned back into a red and beating heart.

"Soon it will be summer again," said Gerda, "and we'll see the roses on our rooftop."

"I'm not going to cry," said Kai. "We never cry."

But he did cry. He cried only one tear, but it washed that grain of devil-glass out of his eye.

Then he knew Gerda, and knew how much he loved her, and shouted happily: "Gerda! Gerda! Where have you been all this time? And where have I been?"

Kai looked around him. "How cold this place is!" he said. "How cold and huge and empty!"

And he hung onto Gerda, and they were so happy that they were laughing and crying and dancing all at the same time.

They were so happy that even those flat pieces of ice stood up and danced along with them. And when the pieces of ice were tired, they lay down on the black ice and formed the word ETERNITY.

So the spell was broken. The Snow Queen had promised Kai that if he solved the puzzle he could have his freedom and the whole world – and a pair of skates.

Gerda kissed his cheeks, and the blue-blackness was replaced by the color of roses. She kissed his hands and feet and suddenly he felt well and warm and strong.

What did it matter now if the Snow Queen came? Kai's right to freedom was written out in letters of glittering ice. Kai took Gerda's hand. Together they walked out of the enormous palace, talking about Grandmother and the roses on their rooftop.

There was Kai!

As Gerda and Kai walked away from the Palace, the icy winds died away and the sun broke through the purple clouds.

When they came to the bush with red berries, Moo was waiting for them. He brought with him a young female reindeer, who gave them warm milk from her full udder and nuzzled them.

Then the two reindeers carried Kai and Gerda to the old Finnish woman's house, which she kept warmer than toast. There they completely unfroze their bodies and bones.

They rode on to visit the old Lapp woman, who gave them new homemade clothes and a sturdy sled for the rest of their journey.

Moo and his young friend escorted them as far as the Lapland border, where green spring leaves were budding. There Gerda and Kai said fond farewells to the reindeers and the old Lapp woman.

Soon the air was full of songbirds. The forest was bursting into leaf and out of it came riding a young girl, with a bright red cap and pistols on her belt.

Gerda recognized her horse as one of the four that had pulled her golden coach. And then she realized that the girl was Buzzer. The robber girl was bored with the old castle. She had decided to ride north to see if she liked it.

"Good old Gerda!" shouted Buzzer, vaulting down from her horse and shaking hands vigorously. "You found that boy." She hugged Gerda, then turned to Kai.

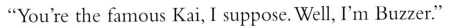

"You're the famous Kai, I suppose. Well, I'm Buzzer."

"What do you do?" asked Kai, shaking hands politely.

"I'm a robber," said Buzzer. "Got any gold?"

"Not an ounce," said Kai apologetically. "Are you really a robber?"

Buzzer narrowed her eyes. "You're a funny sort of lad. I wonder if you're worth chasing halfway round the world?"

Gerda patted Buzzer's cheek. "How are the Prince and Princess?"

"Who knows?" said the robber girl. "They've gone to foreign parts."

"And the Crow?" asked Gerda.

"Dead," said Buzzer bluntly. "That tame wife of his is a widow these days. She hops about with a bit of black elastic round her leg being sorry for herself, but it's all show. So how did you manage to rescue this boy?"

Gerda and Kai told their story.

"Well done," said Buzzer. "I'd better stir me stumps if I'm going to rob this big, rich world. So spit for our next meeting and shake for our friendship."

The three of them spat in their hands and then shook for friendship. Then the robber girl promised that if ever she came to their town she'd pay them a surprise visit, winked, jumped onto her horse and rode away into the wide world.

————————

The forest was bursting into leaf and out of it came riding a young girl.

*They both thanked the river and gulped
a drink of her good water.*

Gerda and Kai walked on hand in hand. They came
to the banks of the winding river, and followed its course for
a time, avoiding the old lady's cottage in the cherry orchard. As they
paddled on one of the river's shingly beaches to refresh their feet,
Gerda said to Kai: "This is the river that helped me find you.
I must thank her." So she sang to the river:

"*Winding river, slowly strolling by,*
I've come back with my good friend Kai.
Winding river, you've been kind to me
As you wander toward the sea,
Let me thank you —"

At that moment, riding on a wavelet, she saw her two red shoes.
She splashed her way toward them and put them on. "She's returned
my red shoes," she told Kai, and they both thanked the river and
gulped a drink of her good water from their cupped hands.

"I like your shoes," said Kai, who didn't usually notice clothes,
as they walked on.

Suddenly church bells rang out.

"I know those bells," said Gerda. "Those are the bells of home."

"Look," said Kai. "There's our town. And there's our rooftop."

Now they started running all the way to Grandmother's door, and up the stairs and into the room, where everything looked just the same as it ever did – all except for a pair of shining skates in the corner.

The grandfather clock was saying, "Tick! Tock!" and its hands moved, but as Gerda and Kai climbed through the window and onto the rooftop, they suddenly noticed that they were both grown up.

The roses were blooming beside the open window, and Gerda and Kai sat down on the stools that they had used since they were little children, and they held each other's hands.

The icy splendor of the Snow Queen's Palace was like a bad dream of long ago. Grandmother was cooking and singing to herself.

Gerda and Kai looked into each other's eyes and understood what they saw there. For a long time they sat, just like grown-ups, just like children – and it was summertime and there was warm sunshine on the roses.

Gerda and Kai looked into
each other's eyes.

Journey to the Snow Queen's Palace

KAI IS PLAYING WITH HIS toboggan in the Square in Big Town when the Snow Queen takes him off to her icy palace. When Gerda sets off to find him she begins a long and dangerous journey. But she meets many interesting people and animals along the way.

The winding river

The Crow

Gerda sets off to find Kai

✳ CHERRY ORCHARD
Gerda nearly forgets about Kai when she stays with the old woman in her pretty cottage.

Big Town Square

Kai and Gerda's rooftop garden

The Snow Queen and Kai's route to Palace

N

E ——— **W**

S

The Snow Queen's Palace

✷ PRINCESS' PALACE
Disappointment awaits Gerda
when the Crow takes her to
meet the amazingly clever
Princess in her
quest for Kai.

Moo must leave Gerda
at the berry bush to go
the last part of her journey
on her own.

Berry bush

✷ THE FINNISH WOMAN
This kind old lady knows
a bit of magic and she
can help Gerda find her
way to the Palace.

✷ ROBBERS' CASTLE
Gerda doesn't know what
will happen to her when
she's ambushed by robbers
in the deep forest and taken
to their ruined castle.

✷ THE LAPP WOMAN
Although the Lapp
woman cannot help
Gerda find Kai, she
has a friend who can.

A Fairy Tale World

HANS CHRISTIAN ANDERSEN is probably the world's most famous writer of fairy tales. *The Snow Queen* is one of his longest tales and one of his best known, but is only one of 156 that he wrote in all! Many of these have become classics.

Andersen surrounded by some of his fairy tale creations.

✳ COLLECTOR OF TALES

As a child, Andersen loved to listen to folk-tales and fairy stories. When he grew up, he decided to try to write down some of these stories in his own words. He wanted to write them as if he were telling them to a child and by so doing he made them come alive to a new audience of children.

The Emperor's New Clothes *(1837) was originally a Spanish Medieval tale.*

The Wild Swans *was a traditional Danish folk tale.*

✳ GRIMM'S FAIRY TALES

The German brothers Wilhelm and Jacob Grimm are also famous for their fairy tales. Unlike Andersen, though, they did not write any stories of their own but collected folk-tales and wrote them down.

Jacob (1785–1863) and Wilhelm (1786–1859).

Their adaptation of Cinderella was very popular.

✳ INVENTED STORIES

Most of Andersen's tales came from his imagination, often inspired by things that had happened to him. The story of the ugly duckling who turns into a beautiful swan, for example, compares with Andersen's own transformation from a poor, and lonely boy into a rich and much-loved writer of fairy tales.

A scene from The Ugly Duckling *(1843).*

Andersen began writing The Snow Queen *on December 5, 1844. Sixteen days later it was published in book form!*

A bronze statue of Andersen's The Little Mermaid *stands at the entrance of the harbor at Copenhagen, Denmark's capital city, as a tribute to its famous citizen.*

Hans Christian Andersen

*Hans Christian
Andersen
(1805–1875)*

THE STORY OF HANS ANDERSEN'S life is like one of his fairy tales. He was born and brought up in Denmark with his parents who were very poor. He was an only child, and he spent most of his time reading and making up stories for his toy theaters.

*Andersen's childhood home
at Odense, Denmark.*

✷ FAIRY TALES

At 14, Andersen went to seek his fortune in Copenhagen. Like Kai in *The Snow Queen*, he was clever, and he won a scholarship for an education. Afterward, he started to write and in 1835 the first of his fairy tales for children was published.

*The Princess
and the Pea
(1835)*

*The Snow Queen
(1844)*

✷ FAME AND FORTUNE

Andersen's fairy tales made him famous all over the world. His stories have been translated into more than 100 languages, and many of his tales have been made into much-loved films.

*Danny Kaye as Hans Andersen telling his fairy
tales to children, in the 1952 film about his life.*